To my valentine, Albert, with all my heart
–L. B. F.

To a very special Ruby
and the fun we all had at Camp Tuffit
–L. A.

Text copyright © 2014 by Laurie B. Friedman
Illustrations copyright © 2014 by Lynne Avril

Carolrhoda Books
A division of Lerner Publishing Group, Inc.
241 First Avenue North
Minneapolis, MN 55401 USA

Main Text set in Fink Heavy 16.5/24. Typeface provided by House Industries.

For reading levels and more information, look up this title at www.lernerbooks.com.

Library of Congress Cataloging-in-Publication Data

Friedman, Laurie B., 1964-
    Ruby Valentine and the Sweet Surprise / by Laurie Friedman ;
illustrated by Lynne Avril.
        pages cm
    Summary: Ruby's pets compete for her affection on Valentine's Day.
    ISBN 978-0-7613-8873-9 (lib. bdg. : alk. paper)
    ISBN 978-1-4677-4619-9 (eBook)
    [1. Stories in rhyme. 2. Pets-Fiction. 3. Birds-Fiction. 4. Cats-Fiction. 5. Animals-
Infancy-Fiction. 6. Valentine's Day-Fiction.] I. Avril, Lynne, 1951- illustrator. II. Title.
III. Title: Room for two.
PZ8.3.F9116Rt 2014
[E]-dc22   2013030662

Manufactured in the United States of America
1 - DP - 7/15/14

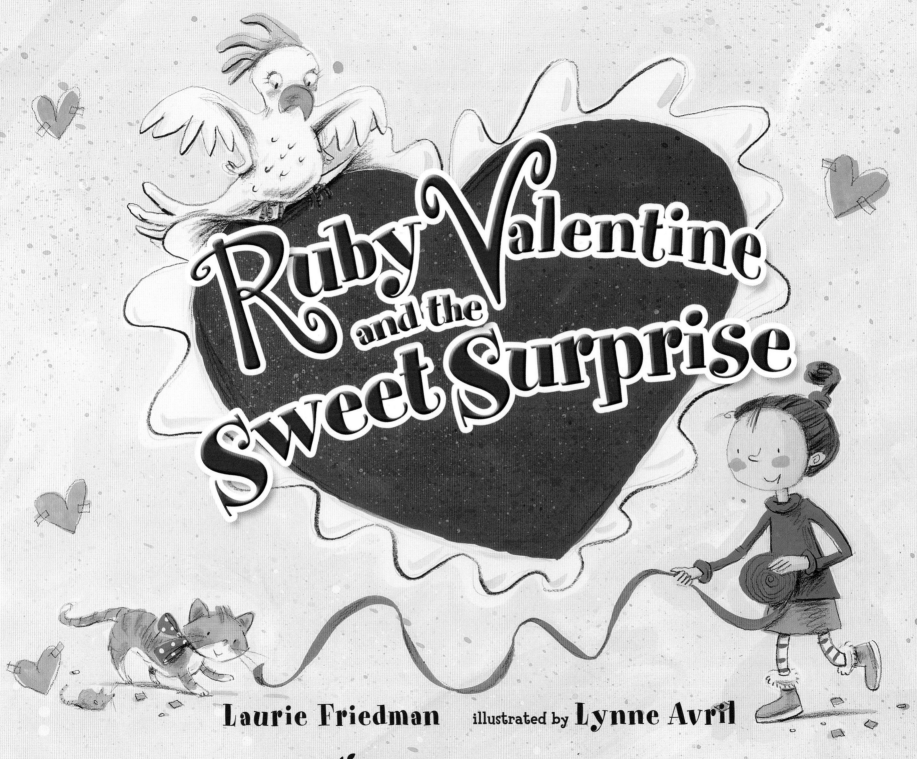

Ruby Valentine and the Sweet Surprise

Laurie Friedman   illustrated by **Lynne Avril**

CAROLRHODA BOOKS MINNEAPOLIS

At the Heartland railway station,
Ruby hugged Lovebird good-bye.
She said she'd just be gone a day—
but what she didn't say was why.

Ruby Valentine boarded a train and took a trip into the city.

When she returned to Heartland,
she brought home a baby kitty.

He was soft and sweet and fluffy,
a precious little ball of fur.
"I'll name you Sweetie Pie," said Ruby.
And the cat began to purr.

Ruby loved her little Sweetie Pie.

She taught him how to play.

She set out bowls of milk.

He grew bigger by the day.

Cute and cuddly in his new home,
he brought Ruby lots of joy.
But not everyone was enamored
with this little feline boy.

Lovebird was not happy.
This was more than she could bear.
Lovebird missed the good old days
when she and Ruby were a pair.

Week after week, Lovebird watched the new apple of Ruby's eye. And she could not help but think:

Lovebird wanted to show Ruby
she was her number one pet.
She wanted to do something special,
something Ruby would never forget.

So as Ruby's favorite day drew close,
Lovebird thought and plotted.
She planned Valentine's to perfection.
Her t's were crossed. Her i's were dotted.

When Valentine's Day arrived,
Ruby pulled her pets in tight.
"I'm going to town to get supplies.
We'll celebrate tonight!"

As soon as Ruby left, Lovebird put her plan in action.
But she had not anticipated Sweetie Pie's reaction.

When **Lovebird** baked a cake and iced it to perfection,

Sweetie Pie concocted a much fancier confection.

When **Lovebird** hung streamers and hearts along the walls,
Sweetie Pie flung confetti in every room and down the halls.

And when **Lovebird** arranged flowers in honor of the day,

Sweetie Pie brought in a more elaborate bouquet.

Lovebird looked around the house.
Her plans had gone awry.
"You rotten cat!" squawked Lovebird.
Then she lunged at Sweetie Pie.

When Ruby returned home,
she was shocked at what she saw.
A mess in every corner,
her pets locked in a brawl.

She dropped her bags of goodies and cried out in dismay:
"Can someone please explain what happened while I was away!?!"

Both pets talked at once,
telling what they'd tried to do.
That's when Ruby told them . . .

"There's room in my heart for two."

Then she helped them clean and dust.
They used mop and rag and broom.

They scoured every corner.
They tidied every room.

They took a nice, long bath.
They scrubbed the day away.

Ruby set out all
her goodies . . .

For a Valentine's buffet!

Then Ruby said, **"SURPRISE!**
There's still more to celebrate.
We're going to watch a movie.
You two get to stay up late!"

So Ruby, Lovebird, and Sweetie Pie
all snuggled up in a chair.
They had to squish together,
but no one seemed to care.

When the movie ended,
both pets looked sad and down.
"Valentine's Day is over,"
they both said with a frown.

Then Ruby hugged her pets and said,
"There's something we have plenty of...

"This Valentine's Day is over, but we'll never run out of love."